How to Outwit Witches

How to Outwit Witches

Catherine Leblanc

Roland Garrigue

INSIGHT KIDS

San Rafael, California

How do you outwit witches who are headed **your way?**

They have crooked fingers, hunched backs, voices squeakier than a rusty gate, long black robes, and pointy hats that are nearly as sharp as their noses! Ha!

Without a doubt, these are the scariest of witches!

Warn them that you know what they are and that they can never catch you!

Sprinkle black pepper on their big noses. It will make them sneeze and back away!

Witches fly about on their brooms,
sneering and jeering. . . .

Go grab the vacuum. . . .
Climb on quickly and **vroom!**
They'll never snatch you!

How do you outwit clever witches?

They might offer you a shiny poisoned apple. . . .

Whatever you do, just don't bite it!
Squish it into applesauce for the worms.

They might open up a golden cage
and invite you to enter,
only to lock you up
until the end of your days.

Show them that you
have good manners:
do insist that they go first!

How do you outwit witches who cast spells?

The evilest witches want to take you
far off into the forest. . . .

They clomp toward you,
casting shadows as they near . . .
but there is still time to escape:
release some mice at their feet!

They'll hitch up their skirts
and run away screaming.
HA!

Witches live with all kinds of creatures:
spiders, crows, bats, and cats. **BEWARE!**

They'd like to turn you into a parrot
to make their zoo complete!

Pretend to be stupid . . .

obey their commands

but sneak into the library:

open their magic books,

discover their magic spells,

and turn them into toads, snakes, or old crows!

If you don't know how to read yet, cut up the pages
and mix up all the words:
they'll mess up all their spells
and shrink themselves by accident!

How do you outwit witches disguised as princesses?

The absolute worst kind of witches
are those who are not always creepy and ugly.
To trick you and trap you,
they can make themselves ravishing and charming!

But their disguises do not last long.
Don't come running when they call
and don't tell them they look pretty.
But watch them closely. . . .

You'll begin to notice the glare in their eyes,
the grimace in their smiles, and the skull in their rings. . . .

You'll recognize who they really are—
they can't bamboozle you!

Witches detest children,
absolutely all of them,
and dream of cooking them in a stew!
Even if they compliment you
and tell you they adore you,
even if they shower you with gifts and gold coins,
it's only to make a better broth. . . .

Save yourself before they can heat up the cauldron!

And help keep other kids from this diabolical fate
by preparing your own special recipe:
stinging nettles, slugs, and pumpkin poison.
It will turn the witches into bottles!

How do you outwit witches during their rituals?

At night,
witches gather around a fire
and dance together,
making eerie music.

Don't be scared, they're not paying attention to you. . . .
Seize the moment and have fun with your friends!
Pour out their potions,
cut up their black capes,
and throw their books and brooms
into the fire!

The witches will see the fireworks
but find themselves powerless!

Without their wands they will scratch their heads,
wail, and run away, too upset to rejoin the party.

If you find a witch in the closet,
quickly close the door!

And if you see one on this page,
SLAM the book shut!

That witch will get caught
between the pages, SPLAT!
She'll be squished completely flat!

The End

For Louane, who hunts monsters, wolves,
dinosaurs . . . and wicked witches!
—CL

To my little sorcerer nephews whose help was
priceless while creating these images.
—RG

INSIGHT
KIDS

PO Box 3088
San Rafael, CA 94912
www.insighteditions.com

Find us on Facebook: www.facebook.com/InsightEditions
Follow us on Twitter: @insighteditions

First published in the United States in 2013 by Insight Editions.
Originally published in France in 2009 by Éditions Glénat.
Comment Ratatiner les Sorcières?
by C. Leblanc and R. Garrigue © 2009 Éditions Glénat
Translation © 2013 Insight Editions

Thanks to Christopher Goff and Marie Goff-Tuttle
for their help in translating this book.

Library of Congress Cataloging-in-Publication Data available.

ISBN: 978-1-60887-193-3

ROOTS of PEACE   ®REPLANTED PAPER

Insight Editions, in association with Roots of Peace, will plant two trees for each tree used in the
manufacturing of this book. Roots of Peace is an internationally renowned humanitarian organization
dedicated to eradicating land mines worldwide and converting war-torn lands into productive farms
and wildlife habitats. Roots of Peace will plant two million fruit and nut trees in Afghanistan and
provide farmers there with the skills and support necessary for sustainable land use.

Manufactured in China by Insight Editions

10 9 8 7 6 5 4 3 2